FLY
AWAY
PETER

First published in the United Kingdom in 1963

This paperback edition first published the
United Kingdom in 2016 by
Pavilion Children's Books
1 Gower Street
London, WC1E 6HD

An imprint of Pavilion Books Company Ltd

ISBN: 9781843653219

A CIP catalogue record for this book is available from the British Library.

10 9 8 7 6 5 4 3 2 1

Printed and bound in China

This book can be ordered direct from the publisher at the website:
www.pavilionbooks.com, or try your local bookshop.

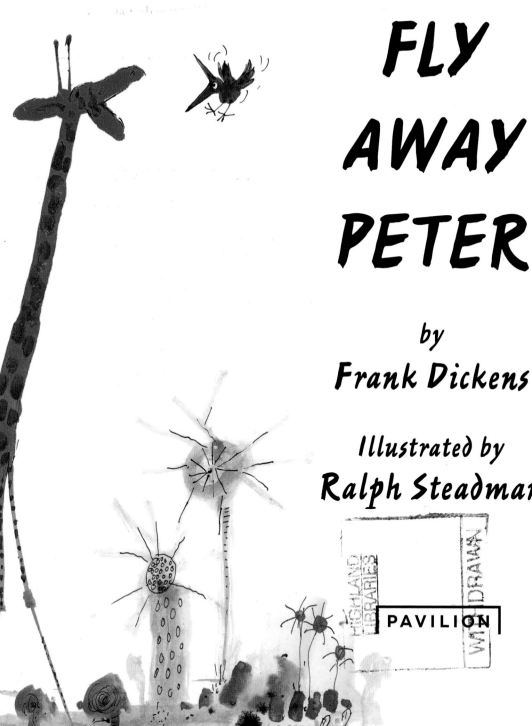

FLY AWAY PETER

by

Frank Dickens

Illustrated by

Ralph Steadman

PAVILION

Jeffrey the giraffe was walking slowly through the forest. Although the sun was shining and it was a lovely day he was very unhappy.

He was unhappy because he was different from other giraffes. He was the same size as other giraffes and had the same spots as other giraffes but he had a short neck and other giraffes had long necks.

Because he was so unhappy
he was not looking where he
was going and almost stepped
on a little bird who was
walking in the grass.

"Look where you are going," cried the little bird. "You nearly stepped on me."

"I am very sorry," said Jeffrey.

"What *ARE* you?" asked the little bird. "You are the same size as a giraffe and you have the same spots as a giraffe but you cannot *BE* a giraffe because you have such a short neck."

"I *AM* a giraffe," said Jeffrey,
"but my neck has not grown.
Because of this I can't play
with other giraffes.
I have no friends."
And he began to cry.

"Do not cry," chirped the little bird. "I too have no friends. Let us go for a walk. My name is Peter."

"What are *YOU*?" asked Jeffrey. "You are the same size as a bird and you have the same wings as a bird but you cannot BE a bird for birds do not go for a walk. Birds *FLY*."

"I *AM* a bird," said Peter sadly, "but I cannot fly.
Because of this I can't play with other birds.
That is why I'm lonely."

"My name is Jeffrey," said the giraffe.
"Let's be friends and play games together. Climb upon
my back and we'll find somewhere to live," smiled Jeffrey.

So Peter climbed on to Jeffrey's back and off they went,
the giraffe with the short neck and bird that could not fly.

Deeper and deeper into the forest they went,
looking for a place in which to live.

Suddenly, in the middle of the forest
they found a small blue lake with
fruit trees growing all around.
"This is a nice place," cried Jeffrey.
"The fruit and leaves hang low and cool
and there is plenty of water in the lake."

"It is a nice place for hide-and-seek too,"
laughed the little bird.
"Hide-and-seek?" asked Jeffrey.
"What is that?"
"Hide-and-seek is a game," said Peter.
"One of us hides and the other
tries to find him."

"That IS a good game," laughed Jeffrey.
"Let's play it."
"I will hide first," said Peter and hid
behind a big grey stone.
"Jeffrey will never find me here,"
he thought.

"READY!" he called.

"This *IS* a good game," said Jeffrey. "I wonder where Peter is hiding?"
He looked everywhere. Behind bushes, behind trees, behind flowers,
behind everything but the big grey stone. Suddenly he spied a rabbit hole.

"I wonder whether he is
hiding down that rabbit hole."
He smiled and put his
head inside to see if
Peter was there.

"No," he said to himself,
"he is not hiding down here."

And then he had a surprise.

When he tried to pull his head out of the rabbit hole he found he could not move it.

He PULLED
and PULLED
and PULLED
and PULLED but it was no use.

His head was trapped
in the rabbit hole.

"What shall I do?"
he said to himself.
"What ever shall I do?"

Meanwhile his friend Peter was still hiding behind the big grey stone.
"Jeffrey is a long time looking down that rabbit hole," he thought.

"Here I am!" he called,
"I am hiding behind this big grey stone."
But Jeffrey could not hear him. His head was still down the rabbit hole.
"I am over here," called Peter and came out from his hiding place.
Jeffrey did not answer.
All at once Peter realized what had happened.
"Oh dear!" he cried. "My friend is in trouble! I must get help."
So off he ran as fast as he could.

"I must go faster!" he chirped. "I MUST GO *FASTER!*" And he began to flap his wings up and down to raise more speed.

FASTER...

... and FASTER...

... and F A S T E R...

... and F A S T E R... still

And then... Suddenly...

HE FOUND HIMSELF FLYING THROUGH THE AIR!

"I can FLY!"

he cried...

"I can FLY!"

And off he flew to get his three brothers who were sitting in their nest. "Look!" said his three brothers. "It is Peter and he is flying! Let's play with him."

"There is no time," cried Peter,
"Jeffrey is in trouble. He needs HELP!"

At once his three brothers flew off to
tell the other animals...
And because animals ALWAYS help each
other it was not long before they were
gathered round poor Jeffrey.

EVERYONE was there.

Elephants and lions and tigers
and monkeys and rabbits and even
a tortoise and a snail came to help.

"We shall have to **PULL** him out," grunted a **HUGE** elephant.

We shall have to **PULL** him out,"
roared the lions and tigers.

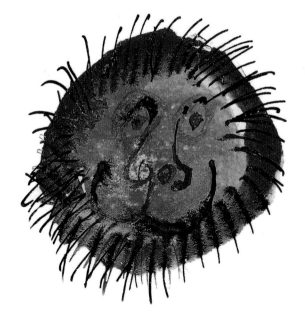

We shall have to **PULL** him out,"
cried the monkeys and rabbits.

We shall have to PULL him out," whispered
the little tortoise and the tiny snail...

So they all began to pull...

"HARDER!" grunted the elephant

"HARDER!" roared the lions and tigers...

"HARDER!" cried the monkeys and rabbits...

"HARDER!" whispered the tortoise and the snail...

So they pulled *HARDER*
         and *HARDER*
             and **HARDER**
                 and **HARDER** and **HARDER** until…

POP!

Out came Jeffrey's head...

And what do you think?
All that pulling had stretched
his neck. It was now as long
and graceful as could be.
"I am so happy," sighed Jeffrey
and looked down for Peter.

"Don't look for me
down there,"
said a little voice
from the sky.

"I am up HERE!"

"**P**eter!" cried Jeffrey happily.
"You can FLY!"
"Yes," laughed the little bird.
"I am just like other birds and you are just like other giraffes."
But when he heard this Jeffrey stopped smiling and looked very sad.
"Does this mean I shall not see you any more?" he whispered.
"Of course not," said Peter. "I will fly over to see you every morning and we can play games all day...
We are friends. But remember..."
And he began to laugh...

"NO MORE HIDE-AND-SEEK!"

THE END